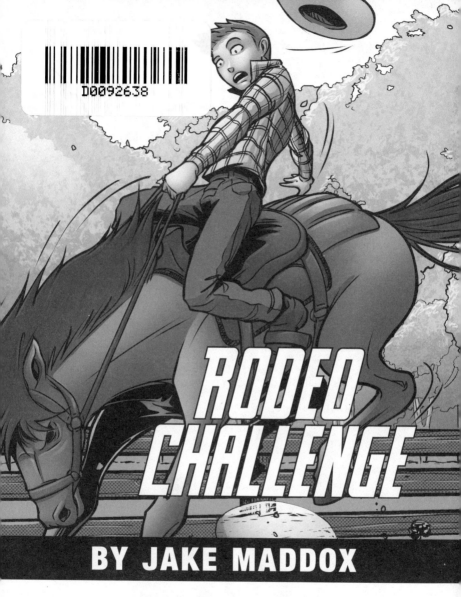

RODEO CHALLENGE

BY JAKE MADDOX

Text by Matt Doeden
Illustrated by Aburtov

STONE ARCH BOOKS
a capstone imprint

Jake Maddox Sports Stories are published by
Stone Arch Books
a Capstone Imprint
1710 Roe Crest Drive
North Mankato, Minnesota 56003

www.mycapstone.com

Library of Congress Cataloguing-in-Publication Data is available on the Library of Congress website.

ISBN: 978-1-4965-5865-7 (library binding)
ISBN: 978-1-4965-5867-1 (paperback)
ISBN: 978-1-4965-5869-5 (eBook PDF)

Summary: When sent to Uncle Hank's ranch for the summer, Wade begins to dream of rodeo glory. Although Wade is athletic, he's got a knack for falling off of horses rather than staying on them. Can Wade find a way to buck the system?

Editor: Nate LeBoutillier
Designer: Brent Slingsby
Production Specialist: Tori Abraham

Printed in Canada.
010808S18

TABLE OF CONTENTS

CHAPTER 1

TOUGH RIDING

Dust hung in the air outside an old red barn. The barn sat on a low hill where two boys watched a girl riding a horse. One of those boys, Wade, leaned against a wooden fence post, his chin resting in his hands.

Wade sighed. "I'll never be able to ride like that," he said.

Javier stood near Wade and clapped him on the back. Javier was Wade's friend and a son of one of the ranch hands. He was also the brother of the rider.

"Maria's been riding her whole life," said Javier. "You just got here for the summer. You can't already expect to be as good as she is."

Wade watched. He was both jealous and impressed. Maria's chestnut brown quarter horse, Sammy, responded to Maria's every word. Sammy dashed, cut, and jumped on command.

Maria rode over and hopped off Sammy's back. She handed Wade the reins. "Want to take him out for a spin?" she asked.

Javier turned to Wade. "That's a rare offer," he said. "Maria almost never lets anyone else ride Sammy."

Wade wasn't about to miss the chance. He jumped into the saddle and flashed Maria a grin. He nudged Sammy with his heels to let the horse know it was time to go.

Sammy didn't budge.

"C'mon, boy," Wade called. "Giddyup."

Nothing.

Maria and Javier were watching. Wade guessed that everyone who was up at the house was watching as well. And there he sat, looking like a fool. Wade gave Sammy another nudge.

Nothing.

This time he reached back and gave the horse a swat on the backside. Suddenly Sammy lurched forward and then danced to one side. Wade clung to the pommel, trying not to tip over sideways. Just as Wade was about to regain his balance, Sammy reared up, kicked, and whinnied.

Wade tried to hold on, but it was hopeless. One second, he was in the saddle.

The next second, Wade flew through the air and crashed to the dusty ground. Sammy trotted off without looking back.

Cupping her hand over her mouth to hide her laughter, Maria rushed to Wade's sid. Javier made no such attempt. He was literally rolling on the ground, giggling so hard that he struggled for breath.

Wade's face turned red. He brushed himself off. He pretended that his shoulder didn't ache from the fall.

"Please don't worry," Maria said. "It's my fault. Sammy doesn't like anyone but me to ride him."

"Story of my summer," Wade mumbled. He swept past Javier and his laughter and marched back toward the house.

CHAPTER 2

OUTSIDER

Wade took a deep breath and exhaled slowly as he walked. The ground crunched under his uncomfortable cowboy boots. Sweat dripped from his hair. His shoulder throbbed from the fall, but mostly his pride was wounded.

The summer hadn't been going like Wade had hoped. Uncle Hank's invitation to spend summer break at the ranch had seemed like a dream come true. Wade was excited when his mom dropped him off.

He imagined doing things like riding horses, roping cattle, and breaking in a good pair of cowboy boots.

But after a month, Wade was upset. The only horse he hadn't been thrown from was an old mare named Molasses. He found he could barely tie a knot much less rope a calf. His cowboy boots were giving him blisters.

Of course, it hadn't all been bad. Everyone at the ranch treated him kindly, and he'd made a great friend in Javier. The boys had become almost like brothers. But Wade could tell that they all thought of him as a city boy. A tourist. He wasn't exactly fitting in.

Wade heard footsteps behind him.

Javier patted Wade's shoulder. "Hey, man, sorry for laughing at you," he said.

Wade noticed the rough feel of Javier's hand on his shoulder, probably made tough from a lifetime of ranch work. The skin on Wade's palms was soft. For some reason, out here, that embarrassed him.

The two of them usually loved to give each other a hard time. But Wade's scowl made it clear to Javier that Wade was in no mood for joking.

"You okay?" asked Javier.

"Yeah," Wade said. "I'm just frustrated."

The friends made their way toward the ranch house. Javier waved to Marco, his dad, who was busy saddling a horse. Marco worked for Wade's uncle, and Javier spent almost all of his time at the ranch.

"Look," Javier said, "I know you had your heart set on entering the rodeo with us. But rodeo's not for everyone."

"Doesn't really seem like I can hack it anyway," Wade replied.

"It's not that," Javier insisted. "I started in rodeos when I was five years old. It's a part of me. It's a part of all of us here."

All of us . . . Javier didn't say it, but what he really meant was everyone besides Wade.

"Yeah, I get it," said Wade. Javier meant well, but his words made Wade feel like even more of an outsider.

Javier socked Wade with a playful punch in the shoulder. "You going to be in the stands tonight? I could use you there to cheer me on."

Wade put on his best smile. It seemed to fit about as well as his cowboy boots. "Wouldn't miss it, buddy."

CHAPTER 3

A PROMISE

The rodeo got Wade's blood pumping. It was the rumble of the crowd as the people filed into the bleachers. It was the smell of the animals. It was the haze of dust that hung over the place. Being there helped brighten his mood.

Wade cheered, groaned, and laughed with the crowd as the events unfolded. He hooted at the kids who happily chased goats around the dirt-covered arena. He and Uncle Hank made bets on who was going to win each event.

"Never bet against a kid with a great cowboy hat," Hank would always say.

Wade's favorite part of the rodeo by far was bareback riding, Javier's specialty. Javier was one of the top youth bareback riders in the state. Watching him ride broncos had been Wade's favorite part of the summer.

This rodeo's bareback riding event came down to Javier and another rider named Travis. Wade watched in silence as Travis got ready to take his turn. Travis tipped his hat, showing off to the crowd.

Wade had seen Travis compete a couple times. He didn't know Travis well, but it was clear that Travis was a loudmouth. Wade secretly hoped that Travis's bronco put him in the dirt.

There was no such luck. Travis rode well. He earned an 85. It was a very good score, the highest score of the night so far.

The announcer called out the final competitor. "Next up, we have Javier Sanchez. He's riding . . . Danger Zone!"

Uncle Hank winced.

"What is it?" Wade asked.

"Danger Zone is probably the strongest horse here," Hank replied. "Javier is going to have his hands full."

Wade and Hank stood up, hooting.

The horse burst out of the chute. Javier held on tight with one hand as the horse began to buck. His other hand waved all around as he tried to keep his balance on the bucking bronco.

The cheering grew louder with every second. Javier was in control. He held on tightly as the bronco tried to shake the rider off.

Finally after the eight seconds that the judges used to score the ride were up, Javier slid off over one side of Danger Zone.

Wade watched the scoreboard. At last it flashed Javier's score. It was an 87, two points better than Travis's score!

"Yeeee-haw!" Wade shouted at the top of his voice.

Hank pumped his fist in the air.

The cheering went on as Javier dusted off his favorite maroon shirt and smiled at the crowd.

Next up was Maria's event, barrel racing. She was the first rider to compete. She sat tall in the saddle as Sammy trotted out.

The clock started. Maria spurred Sammy into action. Sammy streaked across the open field and cut cleanly around the first barrel.

Dust kicked up from Sammy's rear hooves on a tight turn. He and Maria worked together flawlessly. They rounded barrel after barrel.

The crowd let out "oohs" and "ahhs" as the pair approached the final barrel. Maria and Sammy had been on a perfect run.

That's when it all went wrong.

One of Sammy's hooves slipped as he dug into the turn. He skidded through the turn with a jolt. Maria wasn't ready. She spilled out of the saddle and slammed down onto the ground.

Wade gasped. The entire place went silent as an EMT rushed out to check on her. Marco, sitting in the front row, leaped over the railing to be at his daughter's side. The relieved crowd cheered as Maria stood and hobbled off to get further medical attention.

Wade slipped over the rail and stepped around the back. That's where the EMT was checking Maria. Her face was ghostly white and streaked with tears. Wade cringed as he got a look at Maria's arm. It was bent at a horrible angle.

Wade's stomach lurched.

"You've got a fracture here," said the EMT, a young woman with fire-red hair. "We're going to get you to the hospital right away."

Maria's gaze met Wade's. She looked scared and in pain.

"It'll be okay, Maria," Wade said.

"Sammy needs to keep working," Maria said. Her voice cracked. "I need you to ride him. To keep up his training. Tell me you'll do it, Wade. Please."

Wade flashed back to the last time he tried to ride Sammy. He wasn't eager to try again.

But Maria needed him.

"Of course, Maria," Wade said. "You can count on me."

CHAPTER 4

SADDLE SORE

Wade wolfed down a plate full of scrambled eggs for breakfast. He strolled out to the barn. Uncle Hank was out on business. Marco and Maria had gone into town to see the doctor. Javier was still in bed. Wade figured it was the perfect time for him to start working with Sammy. Nobody was around to see him fail.

In the barn, Sammy was in his stall. The horse watched Wade silently.

"Hey, Sammy," Wade called out softly. He dug into his pocket and pulled out a few sugar cubes. Sammy gobbled them up.

Wade fastened a saddle to Sammy's back. Then he opened the gate to Sammy's stall and led the horse out of the barn.

Sammy snorted.

"I get it, Sammy," Wade said in a soothing voice. "I'm not Maria. But we're going to have to make the best of this."

Wade hoisted himself onto Sammy's back. The horse snorted again and shimmied nervously to one side.

"Easy," Wade said. He patted Sammy's neck. "Okay, let's have a little trot." Wade tapped the horse's side with the heels of his boots. He'd watched Maria do this a hundred times. Sammy knew exactly what it meant.

Sammy didn't budge.

Wade tapped a little harder. "Get!" he barked.

Suddenly Sammy surged forward. The burst of movement caught Wade off-guard. One second, he was holding Sammy's reins. The next, he was flat on his back, coughing in a cloud of dust.

Again and again, Wade tried to ride Sammy. Again and again, he found himself with a face full of dirt.

"Fine," he hissed at Sammy. He grabbed the reins. He led Sammy back to the barn. "You win, Sammy. But you won't get any more sugar cubes."

***

After dinner, Javier and Wade decided to do some fishing at a nearby stream. As Wade cast his line into the rushing water, he cringed. His shoulder ached. His whole body ached.

"Didn't go too well with Sammy, eh?" Javier asked.

"That horse hates me," Wade answered.

"Horses can be fussy about who rides them," Javier explained. "Sammy is just upset that Maria isn't riding him."

It was a slow day. The fish weren't biting. But Wade didn't mind, even when Javier thought it'd be funny to push him into the cold water. That quickly grew into a full-blown water war.

After a while, the fishing poles were forgotten, as was Wade's morning with Sammy. The boys stomped through the stream. They launched themselves at each other in a very wet game of King of the Hill.

By the time they headed back home, they were soaked from head to toe.

They approached the house to find Maria on the porch. She picked at a cast on her arm. Wade waved.

Maria rolled her eyes at the drenched boys. "You two," she said.

Wade's face turned bright red. There was something about Maria that made him feel clumsy whenever she looked at him.

"Yeah, well, hey, Maria," Wade stammered. "I'm gonna, umm . . . we're . . . I'm wet."

Maria grinned.

"How'd it go with Sammy?" she asked. Her voice sounded tired.

Wade thought of telling her the truth. But she had been through a lot recently. There was no need to burden her any more. "Just fine," he lied. "We're making progress. Don't you worry."

Maria's face brightened. "Thanks, Wade. That means a lot to me. Maybe tomorrow I'll feel up to going out to watch you work with him."

Wade gulped. The thought of climbing onto Sammy's back again filled him with dread. The thought of others watching him get bucked off made it even worse.

What in the world, he asked himself, *have I gotten myself into?*

CHAPTER 5

UNSADDLED

Sammy reared back and dumped Wade into the dirt for the third time of the morning. Javier hooted. The morning air was brisk. Dew clung to the grass.

"Man, you weren't kidding," Javier said. "That horse has it in for you."

Wade rubbed his shoulder. He picked himself up off the ground. Maria hadn't come up from the house yet, and he wasn't eager to have her watching. "Think I'm done for now," he said.

Javier hopped over the fence. He grabbed Sammy's reins. "I have an idea," he said. Wade watched as Javier unfastened the saddle on Sammy's back. Javier slipped the saddle off and turned to Wade. "Try riding him bareback."

Wade furrowed his brow. "That sounds dangerous, with how Sammy feels about me," he said. "Also, I've never ridden bareback. I'm not even sure how."

"Only one way to learn," Javier replied.

Wade made a face as he looked at Sammy.

"Trust me," Javier said.

Wade had watched Javier do this a hundred times. And riding with a saddle clearly hadn't been working for Wade.

"Okay," Wade agreed. "I'll try it once. At this point, what's one more bruise?"

Javier gave Wade a boost up onto the horse's back.

Everything felt different without the saddle. Wade could feel every twitch of Sammy's muscles. Wade watched as Javier fastened rigging around the horse's neck. Javier pointed to a strap made of rawhide and leather that reminded Wade of a suitcase handle.

"Hold on tight," Javier said. He slapped Sammy hard on the rear flank.

Sammy reared up, kicking his front legs high into the air. This time, maybe because he could feel Sammy's every move, Wade was ready.

He leaned forward, clinging to the rope. Just when he was sure he was about to fall backward, Sammy stomped his front hooves down. Then he kicked his hind legs.

Wade arched his body backward to keep his balance. Again, Sammy kicked, reared back, and bucked again. Wade felt his body sliding to the right, but he didn't let go.

With no saddle between him and the horse, Wade felt ready for Sammy's every move. Sammy bucked again and again, but Wade didn't let go. Sammy gave one final buck — the biggest one yet — and Wade finally lost his grip. He toppled off and landed on the ground with a thud.

Disgusted, Wade brushed off his pants. He braced himself for more teasing. But Javier just stood there, staring. Behind him, Uncle Hank came running toward the fence.

"What?" Wade asked.

"That . . . was . . . amazingly incredible!" Javier shouted.

"Wade!" Uncle Hank yelled, leaping the fence. "How did you do that? That had to be twenty seconds!"

Wade looked from Hank to Javier and back to Hank. He was confused.

Hank broke out in a huge grin. He picked up Wade with a huge bear hug. "That was some of the finest bareback riding I've ever seen!" he said. "By gosh, Wade, we're gonna make a cowboy out of you yet!"

CHAPTER 6

NO TIME LIKE THE PRESENT

The next few days were a whirlwind. One morning, Uncle Hank walked with Wade to the barn.

"The last rodeo of the season is just a few weeks away," he said. "If we're going to enter you in the bareback bronc event, we've got a lot of work to do. It's one thing to have some natural talent. To compete with the top riders, you need to learn some technique as well."

And so it was time to work. Only there was one problem. Sammy wouldn't buck and now seemed fine with Wade riding him.

Uncle Hank scowled. "Just our luck."

"You're a pain, Sammy," Wade mumbled as Sammy trotted through the pasture. "You buck when I want to ride, and ride when I want to buck." He gave Sammy a pat on the head as he dismounted.

Javier, Maria, and their dad walked up.

"You know, old James up the road has a bronco that needs breaking," Marco said.

James owned one of the ranches located nearby. Wade had met him a few times. Even at eighty years old, James still ran the ranch himself.

"You're not talking about that stallion he keeps?" Uncle Hank asked sternly.

Marco grinned. "They call him Demon. Even James won't ride him, and that old man is tough as nails."

"I rode him once," Javier said. "Even managed to hold on for about five seconds. That horse is wild . . . and strong. Wade may be able to ride Sammy, but Demon is something else altogether."

Uncle Hank scratched his chin. "It's up to you, Wade," he said. "If you want to enter the rodeo, you're going to need practice. But it's your call."

Wade didn't need long to think about it. There was no way he was about to get on a horse named Demon. He'd more likely end up with a cast to match Maria's than anything else.

He opened his mouth to kindly decline the offer. As he began to speak, he couldn't help but notice how intently Maria was looking at him. "Let's try it," he said, to his own surprise.

When Wade opened his mouth again to take it back — to explain that he didn't really mean it — another strange sentence came out: "No time like the present."

Maria's smile was almost enough to make it worthwhile.

Almost.

CHAPTER 7

DEMON

James reared back and howled with delight when Hank asked to borrow Demon. One of the old man's gold teeth glinted in the morning sunlight. He looked at Wade with a twinkle in his eye.

"Be my guest," he said with a voice full of gravel. He pointed toward the barn. "There's a first aid kit by the door. Might want to keep it handy."

Hank and Javier led Demon out of his stall. Wade's pulse raced. The midnight black horse radiated power. He had a temper to match. Javier struggled to fix the rigging around his neck.

"You sure about this?" Hank asked. "Your mom will have my head if I send you home without yours."

There's no turning back now, Wade told himself. Hank wrangled Demon into a stall outside the barn. The stall was a tight fit and resembled the starting chute used in competition.

"The first thing you have to do is mark the horse," Javier explained. "Both feet must be in contact with the horse's body as it exits the chute. Up you go."

Wade sighed and said, "I'm ready."

As Wade prepared to mount the horse, Javier held Demon steady. Demon snorted as Wade climbed onto the beast's back and grabbed the rigging. Puffs of Demon's breath formed clouds that rose in the cool morning air.

"Once he's out of the chute, the clock starts," Javier continued. "Control is the key. You've got to hold on with just one hand. The other hand, your free hand, can't touch the horse at any point."

Demon whinnied and twitched. Wade felt the energy building up in the animal.

Javier kept talking, ignoring Demon's growing discontent. "Being able to stay on a horse for a long time is nice," he said. "But it's not what wins events. To win, you've got to be in control. You get eight seconds to show the judges your skill. Ready?"

Wade nodded.

The instant Hank swung open the gate, Demon surged. Every movement combined grace with pure wild energy. Demon instantly bucked — hard. Wade realized that Sammy had nothing on this devil of a horse.

With a powerful kick of his rear legs, Demon launched Wade from his back like Wade was nothing more than a rag doll. As Wade crashed to the ground, Hank rushed to grab the horse's reins.

Javier extended a hand to help Wade up. "You were trying to hold on with your hand," he explained. "That's never going to work. You've got to grip the horse with your legs. Latch on and let your upper body move back and forth with the horse."

The second ride went better.

Wade locked his legs and loosened his upper body. Demon bucked just as hard, but Wade held on, his body rocking back and forth in time with Demon's movements.

It all ended the same way, with Wade face-first in the dirt. But this time, Hank and Javier were all smiles.

"Looks like you're a natural," Hank said. He held up a stopwatch. The timer read 11.8 seconds.

"I didn't even make it five seconds," Javier said sheepishly.

"All right, then. It's settled," Hank declared. "Wade, we're entering you in the Summer Championships. Let's see if you can give Javier here a run for his money."

"All of that assumes that Demon doesn't kill me first," Wade joked.

"Well, yeah," Hank replied. "There's always that."

CHAPTER 8

TOURISTS NOT WELCOME

The night of the Summer Championships approached. Wade continued to work. In the morning, he'd work with Sammy outside the barn. Then he, Hank, and Javier would head over to James's ranch to work with Demon.

In the afternoon, Javier and Wade hung out, talking about technique. They spent hours watching online videos of some of the world's top bareback riders. At night, Wade nursed his bumps and bruises and dreamed of rodeo glory.

A week before the rodeo, Wade and Hank climbed into Hank's pickup and drove into town to register Wade for the event. Maria tagged along to stop at the market along the way.

"Fair warning," Hank told Wade as the truck rumbled down the bumpy gravel road. "The woman who is in charge of registration for the rodeo is . . . well . . . let's just say the two of us have some history."

Wade raised an eyebrow. "History?"

"They were engaged," Maria said. "Now Wanda can't stand him."

Sure enough, Wanda was sitting behind the desk when the three of them walked in. She had a long face and sharp features. She smiled a big smile as they entered. But Wade didn't believe it for a second. Her cold gaze told the real story.

Hank seemed reluctant to approach the desk. Wade had never seen him afraid of anything, or anyone. But it was clear that he'd rather not be here.

"Hank," Wanda said, standing up, barely looking at him.

"Hi, Wanda," Maria said, breaking the tension.

Wanda's expression softened. "I was so sorry to hear about your arm," she told Maria, giving her a warm hug. "How are you doing?"

"It's not so bad," Maria answered. "Not being able to ride is the worst part. But I'm looking forward to watching from the stands."

"To root for Javier?" Wanda asked.

"Well, of course, but not just for Javier," Maria said.

Hank grabbed Wade by the shoulder and shoved him forward. "This is my nephew, Wade. I'd like to register him for the bareback event."

Shifting her attention to Wade, Wanda furrowed her brow. She looked him up and down, tapping a finger to her cheek.

"Nephew?" Wanda asked. "Not from around here then? This is a rodeo for locals only. And it's not for casual riders. We're holding a serious competition here, Hank. It's not just somewhere for out-of-towners to get their kicks."

Hank didn't back down. "Wade has spent the summer with us. It's his home away from home, and he'll be representing my ranch. I wouldn't enter him if I didn't believe he could handle it."

Wanda shrugged.

Wade could tell she was annoyed. She saw him the same way others did — as a tourist. But Hank insisted.

"Very well then," she said. She turned her gaze to Wade. "Understand, young man, that this is no game. You could be seriously injured. And since you haven't ridden before, you won't have a chance to win any of the season trophies."

"Yes, ma'am," Wade answered. "I understand."

Hank was fuming by the time they climbed back into the truck. "Typical," he growled. "Everyone here just assumes you'll fail, since you aren't from around here."

Suddenly Wade felt very nervous. Would the crowd feel the same way? Would they be rooting against him? A lump began to form in his throat.

"You know, Uncle Hank," Wade said softly. "It's very possible that I will fail. It's possible I'll fail big time."

Hank grinned. He reached out a weathered hand and clasped Wade's shoulder. "You're not going to fail, Wade. And if you do, we'll all love you just the same. But I'd rather you succeed, if for no other reason than to make Wanda eat her words."

"Don't worry, Hank," Maria said. "Wade's gonna do great.

Wade couldn't wipe the grin off his face.

CHAPTER 9

STEPPING INTO THE DANGER ZONE

"You doing all right in there?" Maria's voice sounded muffled through the closed door of the men's locker room.

"Yeah," Wade answered, though he wasn't really sure. He'd had butterflies in his stomach all day. But now, here, pulling on his boots and getting ready to compete, the butterflies had turned into angry locusts.

Riding in front of Hank and Javier was one thing. Riding in front of hundreds of strangers was quite another. He could hear the crowd cheering for the calf roping competition in the main arena.

Wade had played sports his whole life, but never in front of a crowd this big. A little voice in his head told him that it wasn't too late to back out.

Instead, Wade stood, shook his head, and marched to the door. "Let's do this," he told Maria. He hoped his voice sounded more confident than he really felt.

Everyone was excited. It was going to be a big night. It was Wade's rodeo debut, and Javier would be competing for the season championship. Javier was already standing out in the hallway, dressed in his trademark maroon shirt.

Side by side, Wade and Javier made their way toward the staging area. A man with a huge handlebar moustache read off the rider-horse pairings. The other riders had gathered around.

"Javier, you'll be riding Riptide," the man said. "Travis, you'll be on Ghost. Wade . . ." the man paused a moment. "Looks like you get Danger Zone. Tough draw for your first ride, kid."

Travis laughed out loud. "You're putting the tourist on Danger Zone? Ha! That horse is going to launch the kid clear into the fifth row."

Travis wandered off, chuckling to himself. Javier slapped Wade on the back. "Don't listen to him. He's just trying to get into your head. He used to do the same thing to me, until he realized that I won't react. I let my riding do my talking. You should do the same."

"Yeah," Wade sighed. "But come on. Danger Zone? It almost doesn't feel like that was an accident."

"Forget Danger Zone. You've been riding Demon for almost two weeks," Javier reminded him. "Danger Zone is a handful, but he's got nothing on Demon."

From the staging area, Wade watched as, one-by-one, the riders took their turns. Several put up good scores while others found themselves in a dusty heap. It all came down to the final three riders: Travis, Javier, and Wade.

Travis came out of the gate strong. Ghost was a sleek white horse with a powerful kick. For the first several seconds, it was nearly a perfect ride. Travis kept his free hand in the air as he rocked back and forth in time with the horse. At the last moment, he bobbled, letting his feet come off of the horse's flank for a split second. Travis's score flashed on the scoreboard. An 86.

The crowd let out an "oooh."

Javier was next. "Good luck," Wade shouted as Javier set his feet. The season standings between Travis and Javier were neck-and-neck, with Travis just a bit ahead. The title depended on this final event. Javier was simply going to have to be nearly perfect.

Riptide charged out of the chute in a frenzy. He bucked like a horse on fire. Javier was ready for every buck, keeping in time with every move Riptide made.

"YEAH!" Wade shouted as Javier's eight seconds were up. The ride was flawless. The crowd erupted as his score popped up. It was a 90, enough for the championship!

Javier smiled and tipped his hat as he hustled back to the staging area.

"Awesome, man," Wade said.

"Thanks," Javier said. "Look, Wade. You shouldn't even worry about your score. All you have to think about is staying on that horse. No matter what happens, we're all really proud of you."

When it was his turn to ride, Wade shook his arms, trying to loosen up. He closed his eyes to concentrate.

Travis's distant voice broke Wade's focus. "Watch this, everyone," said Travis. "You're about to see a tourist get bucked right out of the arena."

Wade wanted to put it out of his mind. He tried not to take the insult — *tourist* — personally. But the way Travis said it got under Wade's skin.

"You're up, kid," said the man with the handlebar moustache. "You ready?"

Not even close, Wade thought.

CHAPTER 10

MAKING HIS MARK

As he mounted up, Wade felt the muscles in Danger Zone's back twitch. The horse seemed about to burst with energy.

Wade couldn't help but hear Travis's voice echoing over and over through his head. *That horse is going to launch the kid clear into the fifth row.*

Wade made his mark, setting his feet for the start of the run. He'd have to keep them locked there until the horse's hooves came down for the first kick.

The seconds crept by.

Wade's heart pounded. The sound of the roaring crowd was like thunder in his ears.

The chute opened. Danger Zone was out in a flash. In that instant, everything else disappeared. There was no crowd. No judges. No Travis. No Javier. There was just Wade and the horse. Nothing else existed, outside that tiny bubble.

Danger Zone came down hard on his front legs. Wade let his body flow with the horse's movement, using his free hand to keep himself balanced.

Danger Zone reared back and then rocked forward again. The horse didn't have Demon's raw strength. But his movements were much quicker and more fluid.

Wade wasn't quite ready to match its rhythm. He felt his body toppling.

Barely a second into his ride, Wade was about to fly off.

No! Wade told himself.

He latched on tight with his legs, scarcely holding on as Danger Zone's hooves came down hard, and he started another buck. This time, Wade was ready. He let his body fall back, then forward, matching the horse's rhythm.

And so it went, in what felt like slow motion. Every kick and buck was stronger than the last. But Wade was fully determined, and he had the rhythm now.

He dimly heard the tone that told him that his time was up, and he slid none too gracefully off the bucking bronco as handlers came to lead Danger Zone away.

For a moment, the arena was silent.

Wade scanned the crowd. He spotted Uncle Hank and Maria in the stands. He did a double-take as he noticed who was sitting next to Maria.

It was his mother!

She must have come early to surprise him! Together, the three of them started clapping and cheering.

In an instant, the cheer spread throughout the arena.

The rolling, booming noise filled Wade's ears and sent chills up and down his spine. The noise only grew louder as Wade's score flashed up: 88.

Wade stared in disbelief.

An 88! On the first ride of his life!

Javier rushed out and wrapped him up in a huge bear hug.

"No way!" Javier shouted. "You did it!"

"We did it!" said Wade.

The cheering went on and on. For the first time since arriving, Wade didn't feel like a tourist at all.

He felt like a cowboy.

ABOUT THE AUTHOR

Matt Doeden began his career as a sportswriter. Since then he's spent almost two decades writing and editing hundreds of children's fiction and nonfiction books. Darkness Everywhere: The Assassination of Mohandas Gandhi was listed among 2014's Best Children's Books of the Year from the Children's Book Committee at the Bank Street College of Education. Doeden lives in Minnesota with his wife and two children.

ABOUT THE ILLUSTRATOR

Arburtov works as a colorist for Marvel Comics, DC Comics, IDW Publishing, and Dark Horse Comics and as an illustrator for Stone Arch Books. He lives in Monterrey, Mexico, with his lovely wife, Alba, and his crazy children, Ilka, Mila, and Aleph.

GLOSSARY

bareback (BAIR-bak)—referring to a horse, or riding a horse, without a saddle on

bronco (BRONG-Koh)—a wild, spirited horse that has not been trained

bucking chute (BUK-ing SHOOT)—a narrow, metal enclosure for holding or restraining livestock

double-take (DUH-buhl TAYK)—a delayed reaction, usually to something unexpected

pommel (PUHM-uhl)—the upward-curving knob on a saddle in front of a rider

quarter horse (KWAR-tuhr HORSS)—a horse of small, stocky breed that is agile and fast over short distances, such as a quarter mile

rawhide (RAW-hide)—untanned cattle skin

rear up (RIHR UP)—when a horse leans back on its hind legs and raises up its front legs

reins (RAYNS)—a long, narrow strap attached at one end to the mouth of a horse that is used in communicating direction

rigging (RIG-ing)—a system of ropes, cables, or chains

whinny (WIN-ee)—a gentle, high-pitched sound made by a horse

DISCUSSION QUESTIONS

1. Do you think it was wise of Uncle Hank to let Wade ride Demon? Should he have been more careful? Why or why not?

2. When Maria asks Wade how Sammy's training is going, Wade lies. Why does he do this? Discuss what you think guided his decision.

3. Travis picks on Wade, calling him a "tourist." But Wade outscores Travis on his very first ride. How do you think Travis reacted to that? Was he mad? Surprised? Embarrassed? Discuss how Travis might have felt about the final results.

WRITING PROMPTS

1. Imagine that Sammy never bucked Wade off of his back in the opening chapter. How might that have changed Wade's story? Do you think he would have still managed to ride in the Summer Championships?

2. Wanda doesn't think entering Wade in the rodeo is a good idea. Write a paragraph or two of the story from her perspective. How did she feel when Hank introduced Wade? What was going through her mind?

3. Wade's mom never told him that she was coming early to watch him in the Summer Championships. Write a paragraph explaining why she might have kept it secret.

MORE ABOUT THE RODEO

The term *bronco* comes from Spanish, meaning "rough" or "wild."

Rodeo broncos aren't really wild. They're domesticated horses that have been trained to buck when ridden.

The term *rodeo* wasn't widely used until around the 1920s. Before that, such events were often called "cowboy contests."

One of the most famous rodeo broncos that ever lived was named Midnight and lived in the 1920s. Cowboys called the horse unridable.

Some animal rights groups label rodeos as cruel to animals. Modern rodeos go to great lengths to ensure the safety of both riders and the animals.

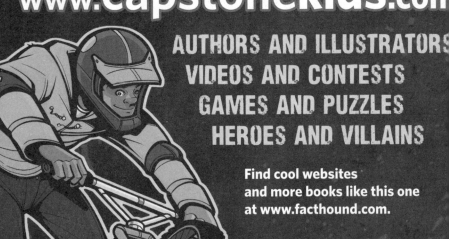